Anna the Moonbeam

For Ivy Sienna Hart, special first
granddaughter for Pops, with lots of love

Special thanks to Sue Mongredien

No part of this work may be reproduced, stored in a retrieval
system, or transmitted in any form or by any means, electronic,
mechanical, photocopying, recording, or otherwise, without written
permission of the publisher. For information regarding permission,
write to Rainbow Magic Limited c/o HIT Entertainment, 830 South
Greenville Avenue, Allen, TX 75002-3320.

ISBN 978-0-545-27049-6

Previously published as Twilight Fairies #6: *Maisie the Moonbeam Fairy*
by Orchard U.K. in 2010.

All rights reserved. Published by Scholastic Inc., 557 Broadway, New
York, NY 10012, by arrangement with Rainbow Magic Limited.

12 11 10 9 8 7 6 5   14 15/0

Printed in the U.S.A.   40

First Scholastic Printing, July 2011

Anna
the Moonbeam
Fairy

by Daisy Meadows

SCHOLASTIC INC.

New York   Toronto   London   Auckland

Sydney   Mexico City   New Delhi   Hong Kong

The Night Fairies' special magic powers
Bring harmony to the nighttime hours.
But now their magic belongs to me,
And I'll cause chaos, you shall see!

In sunset, moonlight, and starlight, too,
There'll be no more sweet dreams for you.
From evening dusk to morning light,
I am the master of the night!

Contents

Mirror, Mirror

It was a cool, dark evening. Kirsty Tate and Rachel Walker stood with a group of children at the edge of Mirror Lake—a wide, still stretch of water surrounded by hills. The two friends were staying with their families at a vacation spot called Camp Stargaze. They were having a wonderful week so far!

As its name suggested, Camp Stargaze was the perfect place to see the night sky. There were lots of unusual and exciting activities for the campers to do every night, too. So far, Kirsty and Rachel had been to a campfire midnight feast, gone firefly-watching in the Whispering Woods, and studied the stars from the Camp's observatory. Tonight, they were about to set sail on a moonlit boat ride!

"Come on, you landlubbers," called Peter, the camp counselor. He led them

along a small wooden dock, and Kirsty and Rachel saw that a motorboat was tied to the dock. "All aboard, me hearties!"

Chatting and laughing, the kids climbed aboard. The boat was lit with lanterns that cast golden reflections onto the dark water of the lake. The boat rocked gently as people took their seats, and Kirsty excitedly squeezed Rachel's hand once they sat down. "Every time I go on a boat it reminds me of the first time we met," she said. "Do you remember?"

Rachel smiled at her. The two girls had met on a ferry one summer when their families were both going on vacation to Rainspell Island. Kirsty and Rachel had liked each other immediately, and had ended up having a magical time together that week — and they'd shared lots of adventures ever since!

"Of course I remember," Rachel

replied. "And I hope—" She broke off as Lucas and Matt, two boys that they'd become friends with, sat down nearby. The girls knew that they couldn't let anyone find out their secret—they were friends with the fairies, and were often called to Fairyland to help on important missions!

Kirsty could guess what Rachel had been about to say— that she hoped they had another fairy adventure that night! "I hope so, too," she whispered quickly. The girls had been helping the Night Fairies search for their stolen bags of magic dust all week, but there were still two bags they hadn't been able to track down . . . yet.

"Everyone ready? Then let's go!" called Peter. A lady named Alison started the engine of the boat, and its loud chugging broke the quiet of the evening. Then the boat moved slowly away from the dock and across the dark water.

"This lake is called Mirror Lake," Peter told everyone, "because in the daytime,  the water is usually so smooth and calm, it's like looking in a mirror. The moon is supposed to be pretty full tonight. I was hoping we'd get a wonderful reflection in the water, but right now it's too cloudy." He shrugged. "Hopefully the clouds will disappear soon, so we can see the moon. Its reflection looks amazing in the lake—twice as bright as it is in the sky!"

It didn't take long for the boat to reach the other side of the lake, where Alison and Peter tied it to a small dock, then helped everyone ashore.

"Wow, look at these rocks," Matt said, shining his flashlight on them. "They're really glittery, aren't they?"

"I think they're granite," Rachel said, switching on her flashlight so she could see better. Kirsty fumbled in her pockets for her own flashlight, but couldn't find it. "That's weird," she muttered to herself. "I'm sure

I had it earlier."

"Okay, listen up," Peter called.
"Tonight's activity is sending Morse
code signals! Morse code is a way of
communicating with someone else using
short and long signals that represent
letters of the alphabet. I'll split you
into two teams, and you'll each have
a special light for signaling each other
across the lake. I'll also give you a copy
of the Morse code alphabet."

Rachel and Kirsty
smiled at each
other. This
sounded like fun!

"Rachel, Kirsty,
Lucas, Matt—you
can be one team," Peter said.
"I'll take you to your base, farther

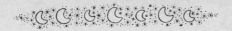

down the shoreline."

"And Hannah, Holly, Tom, and Ben, you're the second team," Alison said. "Follow me, guys, and we'll go in the opposite direction."

Alison's team went on the path that headed to the top of the lake, while Peter's team took the path that went down the shoreline. After a few minutes, Peter stopped walking and stared up at one of the hills. "That light isn't usually up there," he said, sounding confused. "Some people must be camping there, I guess."

Rachel and Kirsty turned their heads and gazed up to see what he meant. Beaming down from the nearest hilltop was a large light that was so bright and powerful, it made them both blink and look away.

"I hope that doesn't get much brighter,"
Peter said. "It could disturb the wildlife."
He shrugged. "With any luck, they'll
turn it off soon."

They continued walking around the
lake until they reached a spot where the
path widened, and some logs had been
arranged in a semicircle. "Here we are,"
Peter said, setting the lantern on a flat
rock overlooking the lake.

Just then, they saw a flash of light from across the water, then another, then another. "Aha!" he said. "Perfect timing. That's the other team letting us know they're ready to start. Let's get ourselves all ready, then I'll signal back to them."

Peter gave Rachel the Morse code sheet to hold, and Kirsty took a notepad and pen. Then the four kids sat down on the

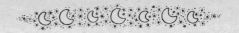

logs. "OK," said Peter, and he quickly clicked the lantern on and off three times. "Now they know we're ready, too, so keep a close watch and let's see if we can crack their code!"

Flashing Lights

They didn't have to wait long before the light across the lake started flashing. First came a long flash, then a short one, then another long flash, and another short one. Then everything was dark again.

"So that was long, short, long, short," Peter said. "Can you find that on the alphabet sheet?"

Kirsty, Rachel, and the boys pored over the chart. Each letter had a sequence of dots and dashes next to it. The dots represented short flashes of light, and the dashes stood for long flashes, Peter explained. "So you're looking for dash, dot, dash, dot," he said.

"There it is," said Kirsty. "The letter C!"

"Good job, and just in time." Peter laughed. "Here they go again!"

They sat in silence while the light across the lake flashed again—one short flash, then a longer one.

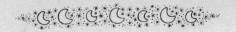

"Dot, dash," Matt said. "Easy—that's *A*!"

There was a pause and then the third letter came. It was a long flash, then a short one, which represented the letter *N*.

It was a lot of fun deciphering the code. After several minutes they had a few words: CAN YOU HEAR THE . . .

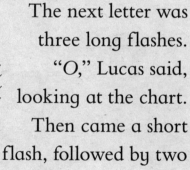

The next letter was three long flashes.

"*O*," Lucas said, looking at the chart.

Then came a short flash, followed by two long ones. "*W*," said Kirsty. She grinned. " 'Can you hear the OW?' Do you think someone is hurt over there?" she joked.

The final letter was a short flash, a

long flash, and then two short flashes. "That's got to be *L*, doesn't it?" Rachel said, running her finger down the chart. "Yes—it is! So their message is, 'Can you hear the owl?' Let's listen!"

Right on cue, they heard an owl hoot in the stillness of the night, and they all cheered and laughed.

"It's your turn to send a message back now," Peter said. "What do you want to say?"

Kirsty tried to think of something funny but was distracted by the light on the hill. "I'm sure that's getting brighter," she said, pointing up at it. "I know, why don't we send the others a message about it? We could ask them if they know what's causing such a bright light."

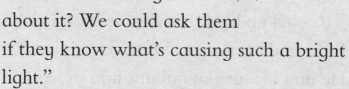

"Good idea," Matt said. They took turns spelling out "WHAT DO YOU THINK THAT LIGHT IS?"

There was a pause, and then the other team spelled back, "WE DON'T KNOW!"

"I can't help wondering," Kirsty

whispered to Rachel as the others deciphered the last few letters, "if that

bright light has something to do with Jack Frost and the goblins. They've caused a lot of nighttime trouble this week!"

Rachel nodded. It was true that Jack Frost had been up to his tricks again. He and his sneaky goblins had stolen the bags of magic dust that the Night Fairies used to keep everything running smoothly in Fairyland and the human world between sunset and sunrise. Since the goblins had taken the bags of dust, weird things had been happening—for example, the sunset had been very late

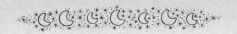

one night, the stars had changed position in the sky, and the camp's midnight feast had almost been a disaster.

Kirsty and Rachel had helped five of the seven Night Fairies find their bags of magic dust, but they really wanted to find the last two bags before their vacation was over.

Just then, they heard a frightened scream. "Help! Help! We're lost in the dark!"

Who's There?

Everyone gasped in shock. "Who said that?" Peter called, shining his flashlight into the shadows.

"It sounded like it was coming from that direction," Lucas said, pointing at a group of large granite rocks nearby. "Come on!"

They ran toward the rocks, which
glittered as the flashlight beams fell on
their surfaces. They searched behind
them, and then shouted into the woods
and up the mountainside, but there was
no reply — and no sign of anyone at all.

"That's strange," Peter said, frowning.
"Let's signal to the others, to see if they
heard any strange shouts where they are."

They wandered back to their signaling
spot . . . but the signal lamp had
vanished!

"Where is it?" Matt cried, hunting
around the rock it had been on. "Do you
think it fell in the lake?"

Peter shook his head. "We would have heard the splash if it did," he reasoned. "And it couldn't have fallen in—there's no breeze at all."

"Then where is it?" Lucas asked. "Do you think someone is playing a trick on us?"

Nobody answered, but just then, Kirsty remembered her missing flashlight and had the horrible feeling that Lucas might be right. Maybe someone *was* playing a trick . . . and maybe that someone was a goblin!

Rachel nudged Kirsty. "Look—over there!" she whispered. "Is it me, or is that granite boulder glittering all by itself?"

Kirsty stared. Yes, one corner of a rock was sparkling very brightly. "That looks like fairy magic," she whispered excitedly. "Come on, let's take a closer look."

She and Rachel tiptoed away from Peter and the boys and headed back to the rocky area. One of the rocks was still glittering and twinkling. As they got closer, they saw that a tiny fairy was perched on the rock, her wings sparkling against the dark sky. "It's Anna!" Rachel said, hurrying over. "Hello again!"

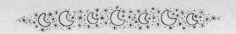

Anna was one of the Night Fairies, and she used her special magic to look after the moon and its moonbeams. She had long, blond hair that was pulled back in an elegant knot. She wore a midnight-blue dress with a pink frill at the bottom, as well as a sparkly cardigan, and a crescent-moon pendant around her neck. Anna fluttered over to Kirsty and Rachel as soon as she saw them approaching. She hovered in midair.

"Hello," she said in a sweet

voice. "I was hoping you'd notice me. I didn't dare come any closer with those boys around, but I've seen everything that's been going on."

"Seen everything? So you know what happened to our lamp?" Kirsty asked her.

Anna nodded. "There were a couple of goblins hiding nearby," she replied. "One  of them called out, pretending to need help. Then, when you all rushed over, he and his friend took your lamp and ran off."

"I knew it had to be goblins!" Kirsty burst out. "Which way did they go?"

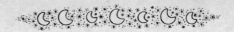

"Up the hill," Anna replied. "I'm sure they're responsible for that bright light shining up there. I'm worried they're trying to interfere with the moon somehow, since they have my magic moonbeam dust."

"Well, we'll help you," Rachel said at once. "But . . ." Her eyes drifted back toward Peter, Matt, and Lucas who were still hunting for the missing Morse

code lamp. "They'll be worried if we disappear."

"Don't worry," Anna reassured her. "I'll work some magic to make it seem like you're only away from them for

a second." She waved her wand in a swirling pattern, and hundreds of pink sparkles flooded out from it, twinkling in the darkness. "There," she said. "It'll only last for a little while, so there's no time to waste. I'll turn you both into fairies, and we can fly up the hill to see what those sneaky goblins are up to!"

Moondust Magic

Anna waved her wand again. This
time, the sparkling fairy dust whirled
all around Kirsty and Rachel. Moments
later, a tingling sensation trickled
through their bodies, and they felt
themselves shrinking smaller and smaller.
Soon, they were the same size as Anna,
with colorful, shimmery wings on their
backs. They were fairies!

"Let's go," Anna said, and she, Kirsty, and Rachel all fluttered their wings and flew up the hill. The higher they flew, the colder it became, and the light from the hilltop got stronger and brighter. As they neared the highest point of the hill, the light was so powerful that they had to shield their eyes as they flew.

"Oh my goodness!" Anna exclaimed suddenly. She stopped flying and clapped a hand to her mouth. Then she fluttered up

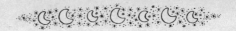

into the sky, not wanting to be seen.

Rachel and Kirsty, who had been flying slightly behind her, flew up high, too. When they looked down to see what had surprised Anna, they saw a group of goblins . . . and an extraordinary creation. Using sticks, pieces of wood, string, an old chair, and pieces of trash, the goblins had built a large disk, with all kinds of flashlights, lanterns, lights, glow sticks, and even glow-in-the-dark stickers attached! Many of the lights were

running with the power from a
portable electricity generator that was
labeled PROPERTY OF CAMP STARGAZE.
Obviously, the goblins had stolen *that*
as well.

"I don't understand," Rachel said,
confused. "What are they doing?"

"I think," said Anna hesitantly, "that
they're trying to make a moon."

"Make a *moon*?" Kirsty
echoed. "But . . . but
nobody can make
a moon!"

"Well, we know
that," Anna replied,
"but I don't think anybody's told them."
Then she stiffened, as she saw one of the
goblins holding a small blue satin bag that
was tied with a drawstring.

The goblin opened the bag, plunged his knobby green fingers inside, then pulled out a pinch of glittering white dust. Next, he sprinkled the dust on top of the makeshift "moon." Immediately, all the lights fastened to the disk blazed even brighter. "There," he said happily. "The brighter the better, right, guys? We'll get rid of the darkness with our beautiful moon."

"That's my bag," Anna said tensely. "And that's my moonbeam dust. We've got to get it back!"

Just then Anna and the girls heard heavy footsteps behind them, and the unmistakable sound of goblin laughter. They crouched low in a bush and pulled its branches close around them as two goblins stomped by. "Look what we got!" one of them bragged. Rachel, Kirsty, and Anna saw him holding up the lamp that had been stolen from the Morse code game. The other goblins cheered. "Good work!" one called. "Let's tie it to our moon right now."

They attached the lamp to the disk with twine, humming cheerfully.

"Jack Frost is going to be so happy

with us," one of them commented. "He's going to love this moon."

"Yeah, and we'll make it bigger and bigger, and brighter and brighter, so it's like a full moon, every night," another goblin bragged. "Unlike the other, silly moon that hardly ever shines very bright."

"Darkness will be gone forever!" cheered the first goblin. "The goblins have conquered darkness!"

Anna shook her head in disbelief. "No, no, *no!*" she sighed. "This is such a bad

idea. It could mean disaster for all of Fairyland!"

"What do you mean?" Kirsty whispered, feeling worried.

"Well, people have got to wonder where this bright light is coming from. Sooner or later, someone is going to climb up here to investigate," Anna explained. "And when they find the goblins, the secret of Fairyland will be revealed. We can't let that happen!"

"No," Rachel agreed. "People from Camp Stargaze have already noticed. Peter, our camp counselor, thought it was caused by campers, but if the light keeps shining night after night, and getting brighter and brighter, I'm sure he'll want to investigate."

Kirsty pointed to the generator that

was whirring loudly as it lit the goblins' moon. "Let's start by taking a closer look at that," she suggested. "If we can turn it off, we can at least put out some of their lights."

"Good idea," Anna said. "Come on."

Very carefully and quietly, the three fairies crept closer to the generator. They stayed close to the ground and ducked behind stones and clumps of grass whenever they thought one of the goblins was about to look their way. Just as they

were about to reach the generator, they saw a goblin put the bag of moondust down on the ground. Then he leaned over the generator to adjust something.

"Even better," Anna whispered. "I'll just fly over and grab my bag instead! Without my dust, their silly moon won't be so bright."

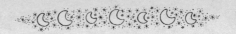

She darted toward her bag, with her
hands outstretched. But just as she was
about to take it, Rachel and Kirsty
saw the goblin pull a large lever on the
generator. The lever increased the power
instantly, and their "moon" started to
shine even brighter.

Anna almost jumped out of her skin as
the light beamed down on her. She flew
up in a panic.

"Hey!" shouted a goblin, pointing
toward her. "There's a fairy! Someone
catch it!"

Caught!

Before Anna could escape, one of the goblins thrust out a hand and grabbed her. "Perfect," he chuckled, examining her. "You're nice and sparkly—just what we need for our moon." With his other hand he picked up a length of string and skillfully tied her to the "moon." "There," he said with a proud grunt.

43

"You can add to the brightness. Best of all, now that you're there, you won't be able to interfere with our plans!"

"You're making a mistake," Anna cried. "Please, let me go. Your moon isn't a good idea, because—"

But the goblins wouldn't let her finish. "Not a good idea? Our moon is a great idea!" one of them told her. "You just look sparkly and keep quiet, all right?"

Kirsty and Rachel, who were hiding behind a stone, clung nervously to each other. They had to rescue their fairy friend, but how?

The goblins started to attach the stolen

Morse-code lamp to their moon, but they soon got into an argument about how they should do it. "We have to think of a plan," Kirsty whispered to Rachel. "We need to trick the goblins somehow. Let's see . . . What could we use to tempt them?"

Rachel was finding it hard to think while the goblins bickered. "We need the lamp to go *here*, to make the moon brighter," one yelled, grabbing it out of another's hands.

"No, you fool, it would be much better on this side," another argued, grabbing it back.

Then Rachel smiled. It was obvious what the goblins wanted most of all! "More light," she suggested. "Anything to make their moon brighter!"

Kirsty nodded. "Of course," she agreed. "So what would be the most dazzling light of all? What would they want to have on their moon more than anything?"

Both girls fell silent as they thought. Then something Peter had said earlier came back to Rachel, about the moon's light seeming twice as strong as usual when it was reflected in Mirror Lake. "The real moon's reflection in the lake will be very bright, if it comes out from behind the clouds," she whispered. "We could convince the goblins to try and catch its reflection!"

"That's a great idea!" Kirsty replied. Then her face fell. "But they'll never believe us if we're fairies—or even if Anna uses her magic to turn us back into girls. They'll know we're trying to trick them."

"Then we'll just have to ask Anna to disguise us," Rachel said, thinking quickly. "As . . . as astronomers!"

"Perfect," Kirsty agreed. "If we look like astronomers, the goblins will think we're experts."

The goblins were still arguing loudly about where to put the lamp, so Kirsty and Rachel fluttered over to Anna and whispered their plan to her.

"Good thinking!" Anna smiled. "And don't worry about waiting for the moon to come out from behind the clouds — I'll use my magic to melt those clouds away."

Anna's arms had been tied down so that she could hardly move them, but she managed to twirl her wand and mutter some magic words. Seconds later, Rachel and Kirsty were their usual size, and they were wearing white coats and carrying telescopes. Their hair was tied back, and they were also wearing glasses. Hearts pounding, they strode in front of the goblins' moon and pretended to study it.

"Marvelous, marvelous," Rachel said loudly. "It's incredible the way this has been put together."

The goblins stopped arguing and turned to see who was praising their creation.

"Genius," Kirsty agreed, looking closely at the brightly lit disk as if she were an expert. "Whoever made this is very smart. Very smart indeed."

The goblins looked delighted by her words. "Well, yes, we *are* smart," they said happily.

"Although . . ." Rachel frowned. "Speaking as an astronomer, I'd say that this moon needs to be much brighter to make sure that the night is never dark again."

"Oh, yes," Kirsty said. "They need much more light here. As a fellow astronomer, I completely agree."

The goblins stopped looking so smug and scratched their heads. "More light?"  one said. "But we stole— I mean, we *gathered* every light we could find. Where can we get more light?"

At that very moment, the clouds around the real moon slid away. The moon's pearly whiteness shone brightly from the sky. And there in Mirror Lake was its mirror image, a full, round reflection that was every bit as bright as the real thing. Anna had worked her moon magic at exactly the right time!

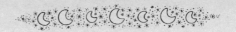

."Down there, of course," Rachel said, pointing at the lake as if it were obvious.

"All you need to do is gather that reflection and your moon will be the best one around," Kirsty assured the goblins.

"No problem!" one of them replied. "Come on, guys. To the lake!"

Moon in the Mirror

The goblins ran off, taking the bag of moonbeam dust with them. They whooped and cheered with excitement.

As soon as they were out of sight, Rachel and Kirsty untied Anna. The fairy fluttered gratefully up into the air, shaking out her wings.

They turned off the generator, which made most of the lights go out. Then Anna turned the girls back into fairies, and they soared down the hillside toward Mirror Lake.

The goblins were splashing around in the shallow water, complaining about their cold, wet feet as they tried to grab the reflected moon. But of course, every time they lunged toward it, the water rippled and the reflection broke up into hundreds of silvery streaks.

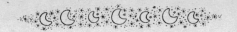

"Those astronomers said we'd be able to catch it," moaned the goblin who had the bag of magic moonbeam dust. Then he glanced up toward their moon and frowned when he saw how weakly it was shining. "Hey!" he shouted, angrily throwing up his hands. He accidentally let go of the bag of moonbeam dust! "Catch it!" Kirsty cried as the bag went flying over the lake. She, Rachel, and Anna all dove frantically to catch the bag. Together, they were able to grab it just before it hit the water. They flew up high and Anna turned the bag back to its usual Fairyland size. The girls grinned. They'd done it!

Meanwhile, down below, the goblins all looked very frustrated. "That's not fair," they whined, stomping back to the shore. "You fairies have spoiled our plan—again!"

"Sorry," Anna said, "but I'll have to spoil your moon, too, by returning all those lamps and lights you took. I know you worked hard on it, but none of those things were yours to use. One moon in the sky is plenty! After all, it is important to have darkness some of the time."

The three fairies flew around the lake, away from the goblins, and Anna turned Kirsty and Rachel back into girls. "Thank you *so* much!" She smiled. "It's great to have my moonbeam dust again. And now, if you follow the path that way, you'll be back with your friends soon."

She kissed the girls — light, delicate

fairy kisses that felt tickly and soft — and they all said good-bye. Rachel and Kirsty both watched as she flew into the dark sky, holding her special bag of dust very tightly.

Then they blinked as a familiar-looking lamp appeared at their feet. It was the one the goblins had taken from them earlier!

Kirsty picked it up and they followed the path in the direction Anna had told them to go. Seconds later, they saw Peter, Matt, and Lucas. Rachel shouted, "Look what we found!"

"Oh, nice work!" Peter said. "Where was it?"

"Just down there," Rachel replied honestly. "Maybe somebody was playing a trick on us, but at least we've got the lamp back now."

"And I know just the message to send," Peter said with a grin. "Who can remember the signal for the letter *H*?"

As they got closer to completing the message, it became clear that Peter was spelling out "HOT CHOCOLATE?" to the other team.

"Now you're talking!" Kirsty said with a smile, as Peter pulled out

a large thermos and some cups.

The other team didn't need to be asked twice, and their friends soon joined them. Then, as Peter poured steaming mugs for everyone, he happened to glance up the

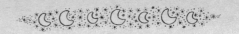

hill. "Oh, look, the light went out up there," he said. "That's good. Everything's back to normal now."

"It certainly is," Rachel said to Kirsty, and they exchanged a secret smile. Helping the Night Fairies was turning out to be so much fun!

THE NIGHT FAIRIES

Rachel and Kirsty have helped Anna, so now
it's time to help the final Night Fairy—

Sabrina
the Sweet Dreams Fairy!

Join their next nighttime adventure
in this special sneak peek. . . .

Nightmares!

"Oh, isn't it sad that this is our last night at Camp Stargaze, Kirsty?" Rachel sighed as she snuggled down inside her sleeping bag. She glanced up at the black sky overhead, where tiny silver stars were glittering like diamonds. "Still, having an outdoor sleepover is a wonderful way to end our vacation together!"

Kirsty nodded as she unzipped her own sleeping bag and climbed in. "It's been fun, hasn't it, Rachel?" she agreed. "I'm so glad we came!"

It was a warm, clear evening and all the children had brought their sleeping bags out onto the grassy area by the tents. They'd had milk and cookies, and Peter, the camp counselor, had read them a bedtime story.

"OK, time to turn off your flashlights now," Peter called. "Good night, everyone."

"I want to come back to Camp Stargaze again next year," said Lucas. He and Matt, two of Rachel and Kirsty's friends, were lying on the lawn in sleeping bags near the girls. "It's the I've ever had!"

"I learned a lot about the stars from Professor Hetty," Matt declared, turning off his flashlight. "And I'm going to keep reading about them when I get home, too. Good night, Rachel and Kirsty!"

"Good night," the girls called.

All the flashlights were off now, and the camp was in darkness except for the pale light of the moon. Gradually, everything fell silent, other than the occasional gentle hooting of an owl in the Whispering Woods nearby.

"Nobody else knows that this has been an extra-magical vacation for us, Kirsty," Rachel whispered, smiling at her friend in the moonlight.

"Yes, we've had some amazing fairy adventures!" Kirsty whispered back.

After the girls had arrived at Camp

Stargaze earlier that week, their fairy friends had asked for them to help once more. Rachel and Kirsty had been horrified to learn that Jack Frost and his goblins had stolen seven satin bags of magic dust from the Night Fairies while the fairies were at an outdoor party.

"I know we've found six of the bags," Rachel said, "But there's still one fairy left to help — Sabrina the Sweet Dreams Fairy."

Rachel, Kirsty, and the Night Fairies had been determined to find the bags of magic dust after Jack Frost's icy magic had sent his goblins spinning into the human world to hide the bags there. So far, the girls and the fairies had outwitted the goblins time and time again. They had retrieved almost all of the bags!

"Let's hope we can find Sabrina's bag tomorrow before we go home," Kirsty said with a yawn. "Good night, Rachel."

"Good night, Kirsty," Rachel replied.

A few minutes later, Kirsty heard her friend breathing deeply and knew she was asleep. Kirsty cuddled down in her sleeping bag, feeling comfortably warm and drowsy. She gazed up at the sky, but suddenly she noticed that the light of the moon had vanished. For a moment, Kirsty thought the moon had slipped behind a cloud, but then it reappeared for a second or two before disappearing again. It was almost like someone was flipping a switch and turning the moon off and on, Kirsty thought, feeling confused.

Then she saw that the stars were
moving. They were zooming around
the night sky, mixing up all of the
constellations. It made Kirsty dizzy just
watching them.

Suddenly Kirsty heard a cold, icy
chuckle. It sounded so close that it sent a
shiver down her spine.

"Ha, ha, ha! Those silly girls and their
pesky fairy friends are no match for me
this time!" Jack Frost gloated. "I have
ALL the Night Fairies' magic bags, and
now I am the master of the nighttime
hours!"

"Hooray for Jack Frost!" the goblins
cheered.

"No!" Kirsty gasped. "This can't be
happening. . . ."

Suddenly Kirsty shook herself awake.

She had broken out in a cold sweat and
was tangled up in her sleeping bag.

"Oh, I was dreaming!" Kirsty sighed
with relief. "I didn't even realize
I'd fallen asleep. What a terrible
nightmare!" She glanced at Rachel and
was surprised to see her friend sitting up,
yawning and pushing her hair out of
her eyes.

"Are you OK, Kirsty?" Rachel asked.
"I just had an awful dream about Jack
Frost and the goblins. . . ."

"Oh, so did I!" Kirsty exclaimed, and
she quickly told Rachel about her dream.

"My nightmare was that Jack Frost
kidnapped all the Night Fairies and
locked them in his Ice Castle," Rachel
said with a sigh. "It seemed so real. . . ."

RAINBOW magic™

There's Magic in Every Series!

The Rainbow Fairies
The Weather Fairies
The Jewel Fairies
The Pet Fairies
The Fun Day Fairies
The Petal Fairies
The Dance Fairies
The Music Fairies
The Sports Fairies
The Party Fairies
The Ocean Fairies
The Night Fairies

Read them all!

■ SCHOLASTIC

www.scholastic.com
www.rainbowmagiconline.com

HiT entertainment

RMFAIRY4

RAINBOW magic™

SPECIAL EDITION

Three Books in Each One—
More Rainbow Magic Fun!

■SCHOLASTIC
www.scholastic.com
www.rainbowmagiconline.com

HIT entertainment

RMSPECIAL6